During אין שלאפלאזע נעכט
Sleepless Nights
And other stories

© 2022 Farlag Press
All rights reserved.

ISBN: 9791096677122

English translation © Daniel Kennedy 2022.

Earlier versions of the translations in this volume have appeared in *Firmament, Jewish Fiction.net,* and *Pakn Troger.*

Cover illustration adapted from *The Wave* by W. T. Horton, *A Book of Images* (1898).

www.farlag.com

ANNA MARGOLIN
During Sleepless Nights
And Other Stories

Translated from the Yiddish by Daniel Kennedy

Farlag Press

Contents

From a Diary   11
In France   43
During Sleepless Nights   53
At a Ball   67

אַ קינד זיצט בײַם פֿענצטער.
אין לבֿנה־שײַן שטראָמען די
האָר װי טונקעלער רעגן.
פֿאַרעקשנט און ליכטיק זוכן
די אויגן
װי דורך אַ װאַלד
די אייגענע װײַטע געשטאַלט.

מײַן היים, לידער, 1929

A child sits by the window.
In the moonlight her hair
streams like dark rain.
Stubborn and radiant,
her eyes search,
as if through a forest,
for her own distant image.

My Home, *lider*, 1929

From a Diary
פֿון אַ טאָגבוך

From a Diary

The 5th of July

I APPROACHED HER TODAY. "I want you to tell me everything," I said. "Why? You understand perfectly well why . . . I must know everything about him."

I caught her gaze and felt pity; her hands nervously gripped her silk umbrella, crumpling the fabric. In her eyes I spotted tears glinting, just for a moment, before vanishing.

She didn't seem surprised, but spoke softly and haltingly: "I'll tell you everything, come to my place. Maybe . . . maybe it will spare you some trouble. Come visit me."

Then she added, "but not right now, it's complicated now. I'm leaving tomorrow and I'll be away for a month; come visit me when I get back."

She handed me her address, scribbled on a scrap of grey paper. I slipped it straight into my pocket without looking at it.

Another month, and I'll know everything.

❖

I'd run into her several times before. The first time she'd seemed perfectly contented, until he entered and she became unhappy and distracted. Later, I noticed that whenever she was alone in a place where he was likely to turn up, she'd be nervous, with a downcast gaze and a pitiful smile on her pale face. I knew she was his lover and so I paid close attention to her appearance: a pallid, inconsequential face—one of those unmemorable faces you encounter wherever you go—dull, close set eyes, altogether somehow sombre and grey. I was curious to hear her voice, so once I casually asked her if it was cold outside. Her voice was shrill and childlike; it didn't suit her aging face.

I don't doubt for a moment that he has intimate relations with other women too. But she's the only one I know about for certain. It's as clear as day. The uneasy way she moves whenever she sees him tells me so, along with the guilty, satisfied grin that appears on his lips in her presence—in her presence, in mine and no doubt in the presence of other unknown women too.

And she's also aware of who I am.

She almost certainly knows what binds me to her. We always greet each other warmly, as though glad to see each other. But today I couldn't bring myself to play the part. The words pounded in my head: *I must know, I must know everything*.

And so I went to her.

One more month.

The 6th

A question briefly arose in my mind: "what right do I have to snatch a page of his life that he'd wanted to hide and read it by force, to sneak around, to spy over his shoulder?"

I'm choosing the harshest, most self-critical words: to *sneak*, to *spy,* and yet they leave me cold. I feel no shame, no guilt, only love.

It's my sole response, my sole defence: I am in love—I am lovesick. Not allowing myself to be deceived is making me ill, not being able to forget, even when we are together. In those moments my senses of sight and hearing are monstrously heightened and on edge. Everything he does or says, his every facial expression, is a major event that I mull over day and night. I try to make sense of it, try to dissect it, break it down to its tiniest parts. A false tone or an artificial smile leaves me deeply unhappy. And always in my thoughts of him I hit upon a solid wall—his life, his private world that I'm not part of, that he wishes to keep hidden from me. I stand before it for hours with fixed eyes.

I love—that gives me the right. And if it doesn't, I don't need the right. I'll do what I must because I can't do otherwise.

I can't.

The 8th

I feel unwell.

In these dreadful times I relive an old, beautiful recurring dream. I don't remember if it first came to me in my slumber, or while I was awake.

This is how it always goes: when my life becomes dismal and sombre, I delve into my past and select sparks of pure joy, of untainted happiness and use them to light up my blackened soul.

And here it is, my beautiful dream: A quiet, trembling night spread its wings over the blooming valley, shrouding it in starless obscurity. And in the centre of the valley, a mountain rises up, high and proud, blanketed in snow, its peak towering up into the open skies. Here and there in the valley, campfires flare up, and around the fires, men and women dance in wild, seductive circles. The air is hot and heavy with their sinful songs, impudent laughter, drunken kisses and caresses. I, too, am there, wandering among them, singing and dancing, with untied hair on which gleams a braided garland of red poppies.

But my heart, full of sorrow and yearning, is not with them. My eyes are trained on the snow-capped mountain, on its fog-shrouded peak. And the louder their joyous song rings out, the stronger my sorrow and yearning draws my soul upwards, giving it wings to reach the sky. Quietly, I slip away from the wild circle—no one notices—and I go wherever my heart desires. The darkness and I embrace the mountain—both of us pining for its luminous heights. The darkness reclines by the foot of the mountain, suddenly weak and tired, while I climb to its hidden summit. The wind snatches away my garland. The song resonates down below; I go my way without songs or flowers. And the mountain will not allow me, weak child of humankind, to touch its proud head; it tries to frighten me with chasms and slippery rocks. It tears at my clothing, bloodies my body, wounds my feet. But at what cost to glimpse the earth from afar, to see the sky up close? There's the sky, ever closer, ever closer—you could just reach out and touch it!

Yearning conquers fear. Down below, the daytime fires still smoulder. The first rays of the rising sun gently fall on my trembling body, on the hard snow that envelopes the summit.

The 9th

Yesterday I was so intoxicated by my own dream I had to stop writing. But today I feel like I've been carried high over the earth. As though my recent suffering has grown milder and paler.

The 11th

I just want to know what sweet words he said to her: the same ones he said to me? Or did she inspire different words in him? Did he pursue her? Did he tell her he was sick with passion, that he needed no one else but her?

I just want her to tell me. Nothing more.

❖

Reality and dreams are weaving together, flowing into each other and I don't know where one ends and the other begins.

I am a queen . . . What? Is it hard to imagine that I'm a queen? I sit now in the sombre throne room and I have allowed her, my lady-in-waiting, to sit by my side.

With a stony smile I bid her tell her story. And the lady-in-waiting (her face ashen, her eyes dull) recounts in a low voice, with frequent pauses, how the great artist sought her love, telling her that he was sick with passion, that he needed no one but her.

I listen, cold and proud, playing absentmindedly with my diamond encrusted diadem, so that no one should see how the queen suffers. But she continues her story: how hot his kisses were, how gently he caressed her, what words of love he found for her. And I give her a sign to stop. She falls silent and, bowing deeply, leaves the hall. The cold, proud smile lingers on my lips, and my hands continue to play with the diadem: no one must see how the queen suffers.

So childish! So ridiculous! I'm no queen—I'm a tired child with big dreams. She is no lady-in-waiting, she's a poor working girl. He is no artist.

I know she'll tell me everything, but that knowledge does not make it any easier. It's hard to contemplate. If only the impossible were possible—if only he would come to me himself and confess everything.

I choke up with tears.

The 14th

My books, my great friends, gaze down on me with quiet resentment, calling me to them.

The 15th

He wasn't alone when I met him today. His acquaintance, in the few minutes he spent with us, mentioned her name in passing among others. When we were alone he said: "She is a very important friend," even though I had not asked him anything. And what does he tell her about me? Perhaps with the same defensive expression: "she is a very valuable worker."

I feel sorry for him. How much he has to strain, how many lies he has to tell for me to consider her "*an important friend*" and her me "*a valuable worker,*" and we are not even the only unfortunates.

Sometimes it seems to really pain him, he seems to feel genuinely guilty that on account of petty desires he has shattered young lives in bloom and mutilated young souls.

I feel sorry for him.

The 17th

I have returned to my books. I've been working a great deal today, to the point of intoxication.

Night

Once again, I'm delving into my work with elation. I'm young and strong and not afraid to stare my sorrow in the eyes, drinking it down to the dregs. And because I am young and strong the work draws me in, just as life does, the joy of life.

Lately I find myself pausing in wonder when faced with the creations of the long-gone, half-forgotten peoples. The past is becoming as familiar and dear to me as the present, as the advance fulfillment of tomorrow. I sometimes feel as though I'm bathing in the light of those stars, long dead, which continue to send us their bright, shining light. We are bound to them by thin threads, spun from gold.

The 24th

I sometimes dwell on the fact that there's one thing that time and humankind will not be able to take away from me, leaving me rich, richer than Croesus: the bliss that I derive from a Heine poem, from a Beethoven sonata or a DaVinci painting.

The 25th

No sooner does one rise a little above one's own petty joys and pains, than crystal clear wellsprings of new joy and new pain open up. One watches humanity and its bitter struggle against mortality, its feverish ambition to transcend the frontiers of the possible, to gain access to the mysterious and eternal, embracing it with steady arms.

Is it not like an eagle that rises above fog and cloud, ever higher and higher to touch the sun's fiery bosom with its mighty wings, to feed on its eternally flowing light?

Is it not like . . .

No, not like that, I have no desire for rhetoric, for platitudes, and cannot find the words as deep and great as my awe for mankind, as my awe for its creation. Not with words—I will prove it with my life.

I want to prove it with my life, my brain, my nerves . . . all of my force I will devote to my work.

And I am not deceiving myself about my abilities; I am not overestimating myself.

If my idea is weak, it will flare up just for a moment, halting, fearful of every hurdle. I want to select the brightest and most beautiful ideas in generations, ideas which have until now only revealed themselves to a select few, and make them clear and comprehensible for thousands and tens of thousands of people. May those thousands, tens of thousands, warm themselves in the same sun that shines for me, may they enjoy the same happiness that has been lavished on me.

The 27th

In the last few days I've almost completely forgotten about the address, not forgotten exactly, just not thought about it. Today the whole scene suddenly came to the surface of my memory: how I went to her, asking her to tell me everything . . . The blood rushed to my face, and I was ashamed to face my books.

I must forget it, for a while at least, in order to feel pure. I must work.

The 28th

I sit with my books all day. But then the evening comes, quiet, nostalgic and sad and, unnoticed, the work slips away out of my hands. I suddenly get the urge to see wide, open skies and dark earth, the urge to breathe freely and not suffocates under heavy stones. Here in the long, narrow streets between high walls, you won't find wonders such as these.

I throw myself down on the bed, close my eyes and my fantasy takes me away to where the sky is broad and wide and the earth is free to breathe—to my poor Lithuania.

My poor Lithuania. A sickly-pale summer's evening has already descended on one of its ancient, pensive towns, descended calmly and quietly so as not to disturb the town in its sad musings. With shimmering moonlight it pours down the broad road that leads into the dark, green fields, with their scattered many-branched trees. There's no one to be seen, no passing cart, no birdsong: everything is mute. And I feel ill. A long expected unhappiness has caught up with me. Too heavy for my shoulders—impossible to carry over. I need to hide it deep down so that no one should see it, not even the all-seeing sky. I cut across the wide road and walk towards the grassy field, where the trees rock sorrowfully. Without tears, without words, I fall upon the damp, well-trodden earth, so many others having already passed through it to reach the stooping tree, which has known so many storms and thunder. I snuggle up to them—my companions in grief. Everything is mute, as though a shadow of great suffering has passed over the heavens, fluttered down onto the earth, touching it lightly, passing through for a while, causing the heavens, the people and the earth to pause in astonishment at the magnitude of the suffering and then to fall silent. The silence embraces me in its tender arms, gently kissing my astonished soul and telling of strange worlds where silence and silence alone is the ruler. And not far from me, in bright rows, lie the houses of my town I recognise my mother's house among them. I know that there's no light on inside—no one is home. My mother has long passed over to the other side of the sea. I know that the window is open and beside it stands my mother, old before her time, anger and sorrow frozen on her face. And I know that she is gazing towards the dark field, towards the old trees that robbed her of her child. Her gaze calls out and beckons, demands, and beseeches. I cannot heed its call. In mute sorrow I arise. I walk across the wide road, bathed in shimmering light, toward the houses of the sleepy town, to the window where my angry, forever-sad mother stands.

❖

Child, you dream too much. You must not—it interrupts the work.

The 30th

My days pass in learning and contemplation. I write a lot in the evenings. I'm beginning to have faith in my youth, and in my will.

The 4th of August

I have to go to her tomorrow. It weighs on me, weighs on me like a heavy burden. I don't like the whole thing. Not one bit.

But yes, I'll go. A promise is a promise.

The 5th

I tore up the address, just went ahead and tore it up.

It was this morning. I got dressed to go to her. I'd promised after all. I found it so difficult. My head was spinning. I took out the grey note to check the street number. I looked carefully at the uneven, childish letters and simply did not see, as though my eyes had been covered in a fog. I don't know how it happened, but I thoughtlessly tore it up, tossing the pieces out the window.

Now I can breath easily and freely. But I'm ashamed. I'm ashamed to face myself: how could I have done it? How could I even think of doing it? My face burns with shame.

The 8th

I met them both today. She regarded me with cold animosity. And he, with a guilty smile.

I don't know if they read in my gaze the love and compassion that it imparted. I wanted to approach the poor girl, embrace her like a sister, and find words that would awaken joy and pride in her. I wanted to look deep into his weary eyes and tell him that I felt sorry for him. That he should not be surprised—I pity him. And that he should never feel guilty about me. For even if he brought me the worst unhappiness, even if he should cause my soul to age terribly, there's one thing that he could never kill inside me— my striving for higher things, my ardent longing for the mountain peak.

Signed: Khave Gross, 1909

In France
דאָרט אין פֿראַנקרייך

In France

EVERY EVENING he comes home to his large, disquieting room, drinks tea, and talks with his daughter.

He has a wife living in a small village somewhere whom he only thinks of when it's time to send money. But his daughter, a girl of seventeen, lives with him in the city. He loves his little one very much, and they live together like intimate friends.

He usually comes home a little tired, a little dissatisfied. The disturbing expanse of the room, coupled with the fact that the girl is troubled and distracted, only serves to heighten his discontent.

"You should have made the tea; you know what time I usually come home," he says, irritated.

She approaches, kisses him on the brow—her usual trick to lighten his mood—and sets to preparing tea.

In these moments he prefers not to speak. He looks over the newspapers indifferently, paces around the room, and softly hums an aria from Il Trovatore or La Traviata—he adores "good old Verdi," as he calls him.

Afterwards he turns to the cheap mirror that hangs on the wall and gazes at his reflection with long fascination.

"Another grey hair," he invariably remarks.

The girl works sadly and absent-mindedly. At her father's words an ironic smile flashes on her lips and then vanishes.

The conversation now turns around the same old themes as always: about his young years which flew by so quickly; and about cursed old age which draws ever closer.

"Little one,"

"Yes, Papa?"

"How is it that I've aged so much in the last few years?"

She looks attentively at his handsome yet weary face, at his kindly eyes which no longer sparkle as they once did, at his fair hair which grows ever thinner and says, uncertainly:

"I don't think you have aged all that much."

This vexes him: "Oh, You don't think so?" he throws her words back at her.

She feels pity for her father who is so afraid of growing old, though that fear is alien and incomprehensible to her, and she says, entirely convinced by her own words:

"No, of course I don't think so."

He drums his fingers nervously over his glass. He still does not believe her, but he cannot keep silent for long and so he speaks again:

"Do you know, I bumped into Madam X today. You remember her, don't you? (No. The girl does not remember her) Well, she was in love with me before I married your mother. (A flash of pain darkens the girl's face for a moment) Fret not, my little one, you have nothing to worry about . . . I hadn't seen her in about three or four years. So of course I remove my hat and take a little bow. She stares at me in surprise. It was only afterwards I realised she had not recognised me. 'You've aged so, so much!' she told me. Later I had a hearty laugh about the whole encounter."

In the distance the sun is going down in a sea of flames. The sunset is not visible from their room; the window faces a blind wall of red brick. But one can see the roof of the building opposite, and the spire of the old church behind it, burning gold and purple. Above is a patch of sky, but this has already turned grey, cold and deeply calm. Slowly, slowly, as though embarrassed, long, soft, dark shadows crawl in through the open window, stealing their way into the room, growing bold, and making themselves comfortable in every corner. And, whether because the sun is dying or because her father's words ring with poorly hidden anguish, the girl grows sorrowful, very sorrowful. Pouring him a second glass of tea, she speaks softly, with sincere tenderness:

"It's ridiculous. I mean really. You? Aged?"

"I don't understand either," he says earnestly, "A man over forty is in his prime. When can one live if not now? When does one know how to live if not in these years? It's not with twenty, but with forty that one comes into one's true youth. In France they understand these things.

Whenever they speak, the conversation invariably turns to France. And once they have reached this point in the discussion it is hard to steer it elsewhere.

The father daydreams about that happy land where youth is in no hurry to slip away, where old age tarries long before stepping over the threshold, and where the people know how to live and enjoy themselves.

The girl, too, holds the name "France" dear to her heart. For her it is inseparable from her earliest fantasies about university, her naive girlish dreams of a future life which is bound to be oh so fine, extraordinarily fine! (She cannot stay here after all!) The word awakened images of a great, wonderful revolution, of the great, noble Napoleon whom she had recently learned about, along with memories of the dozens of love stories she's read, which she still pounces on to this day when no one is looking. And all of these thoughts blend and flow into one splendid, rich, fantastic image—France.

In the quiet evening hours these daydreams of education and stormy world dramas fade unnoticed. Instead the love stories rise to the surface of her memory, all half-earnest, gracious, tender and colourful. Forgetting to drink her tea, the girl hastens to recount these stories to her father. And each time, out of compassion for him, she makes the hero a man in his forties.

"He was about the same age as you, a little older . . ."

He always laughs at these "foolish stories," but in the still hours of the evening he listens to them gladly and attentively.

"Of course," he says, "in France that's a commonplace thing."

The sun has not yet died. It only seems that way. With great effort it climbs over the red wall and, in desperation, launches a few sharp bloody shafts of light in through the window, but the shafts are few and weak, they recoil from the dark shadows; trembling and powerless, they fall upon the white tablecloth, and on the young girlish hand resting on her father's bowed head. And in that light, which barges in so unexpectedly she can see with stark clarity her father's weary face and faded eyes; the wrinkles on the wide brow are unmistakable, and the thinning hair, growing silver in the corners . . .

He repeats the words—"In France . . ."

Signed: Khave Gross, 1909

During Sleepless Nights
אין שלאָפֿלאָזע נעכט

During Sleepless Nights

MANY YEARS AGO, when I was still young, happy, and full of life, I used to like, from time to time, to pay a visit to my hometown and see my parents. There I knew I would always be greeted by my father's ardent love and my mother's quiet tenderness.

On one occasion I set off for home feeling ill at ease. I had just received an unusual letter from my elder sister full of vague allusions and riddles. All I could glean from it was that much had happened since last I'd visited. My mother had fallen in love with someone, but the affair was an unlucky one and had come to an unhappy end. Family life had not been destroyed by it—everything remained as before.

I was apprehensive. More than anything I felt a kind of anxious curiosity and tenderness. During the whole journey I thought about my mother. Somehow I now found her easier to understand; I felt closer to her—she had been transformed into a sister in suffering.

I imagined how I would throw myself around her neck, kiss her pale lips and gaze into her deep eyes so that she could not fail to notice that I understood what had happened.

Who knows, I thought, *perhaps in one of those quiet nights she will tell me what caused her such joy and sorrow.*

But as soon as I saw her standing by the doorway of our house my hopes and expectations vanished in the wind.

My mother greeted me with her head held high and her eyes lowered.

I had never seen her so proud before. When I gave her a warm embrace she regarded me with cold astonishment. I released my grip.

At first the oppressive atmosphere in the house took its toll on me. It pained me to see my simple, gentle mother so cold and proud and my father move so feverishly, with such exaggerated attentiveness and cheerfulness.

That's how it was at first. But back then I was young, carefree, and full of life, and this was enough to resist even the oppressive air in my father's house.

I already had a lover at that time, and whenever a letter from him arrived it brought with it light, lustre, and profound happiness, transforming all the days that followed into one long uninterrupted holiday.

I remember one of those days with particular clarity. I'd just been handed a letter from my lover and secluded myself in one of the hidden corners at the far end of the garden to read it. I drank down the words like strong, intoxicating wine; a wave of hot joy enveloped me entirely. I felt like laughing boundlessly, like singing aloud a happy song, like kissing and embracing every living creature.

And when I saw my mother standing at a remove of a few paces, with her upright posture and lowered gaze—so stern and distant as always—I lunged toward her translucent hand. I did not want to see her cold, surprised reaction, so I closed my eyes and said softly: "*Mameshi*, I'm so happy, so happy . . ."

I opened my eyes and did not recognise her. She looked at me with an expression that will remain forever etched in my memory.

She looked at me and yet she did not see me. Pure desperation—without solace or hope—filled her eyes, which in that moment had become so large and obscured that they blotted the bright sun from my view; her pale lips gave a faint smile, contemptuous and without pity . . .

I waited. I felt that a moment had come that would never be repeated; something hitherto unimaginable was about to happen.

"Listen, my child . . ."

She wants to tell me something, and what she tells me now I will never hear from her again.

She placed her hand on my forehead.

"Listen, my child . . ."

I waited a few minutes with a pounding heart: *What is she going to say?*

But suddenly she took back her hand, lifted her head, proud and cold, and with lowered eyes began to speak of some trifle that interested neither me nor her.

But I knew I would never forget the expression I'd seen on her face.

The moment had passed, and, disquieted, she walked away from me, carrying within her an ocean of pain and happiness, a wild storm of conflict and struggle.

Then later, when the dark days came for me and I suffered terrible humiliation and offense—experiencing my great love done in by a mocking grin—I once again went to my parents, to my old home, which had long since grown unfamiliar.

My mother seemed hardly to have changed at all. As before she carried her proud head held high, always engrossed in her own thoughts, in her memories, barely noticing what happened around her. My father had aged terribly, but with the years he appeared to have become both more cheerful and more restless.

Long and sorrowful stretched out the days in my father's house. I wanted to hide my anguish within myself so that no one would see it. I would lock myself away in my room, lying on my white, narrow childhood bed. I would dwell with angst and fury on my own thoughts, speaking to myself and sometimes weeping bitterly. It was only in the evening that all three of us found ourselves together around the large dining table, spending two or three hours in each other's company. And it would often happen that when my father began in his loud voice to recount an amusing anecdote he would fall suddenly quiet. He would rub his brow earnestly, trying to remember what he had been saying, and gaping at us with alert surprise. His attentive, bewildered gaze would long linger on the faces of the two young, women, old-before-their-time, who sat without listening to a word he was saying, each lost in her own dark thoughts.

Long and sorrowful stretched out those days.

When my childhood bedroom grew too wretched for me I liked to hide away in the large, drafty parlour. That room was every bit as forlorn, gloomy, and cold as I was. One time, when I believed I had the parlour all to myself, I sat by the window and with curiousity looked out into the snow-covered garden, at the tall, bare trees; this was in the month of Shevat. Heavy, cold tears fell onto the book that I held unopened in my hands, but the tears did not disturb my view of the melancholy winter scene before me. I do not know how I happened to start singing, though I could never sing at all. Great, strange, hoarse tones burst out from within me, and my song echoed through the room like wild screams. I was lamenting, arguing with someone strong and angry; I wept, pleading for something, demanding it furiously.

Suddenly I felt a soft hand on my burning brow.

And when I lifted up my eyes to my mother I once again recognised that expression of desperation and disdain on her face. And just as before, her lips could barely move; she wanted to say something: "My child."

I could feel that she wanted to reveal a truth that she had carried in her heart all these years. Now I had to hear it. And unable to restrain myself, I asked: "*Mameshi*, what are you hiding from me? Tell me!"

And in that moment everything was lost. Her face once again became cold and severe, though her hand stroked my hair—a gentleness I had not seen from her in some time.

I did not see her again after that. I was not there for her final moments. My life by then had carried me far from my hometown to a strange land among strange people who I attempted through various means to get close to.

Those means, however, did not succeed.

I am now old and weary. Life storms and seethes just as before, casting incandescent yearnings into human souls, summoning them to happiness and suffering, but life no longer knocks on my door: its waves do not reach as far as my threshold. I have already drained my glass to the very dregs. I am weary. My lonely days, my sleepless nights, pass in peaceful silence—without joy, without pain, without desire.

With each new day and each passing night I creep one step closer to eternal peace and calm—to death.

And the closer I get to death the more intently my gaze lingers on my tear-soaked, paper-garland-crowned youth.

During sleepless nights I see, paraded before me, the shadows of those who bore light or shade in my soul, causing it to quake out of love or hatred.

There they all are: with mirthless laughter, with tenderness in their eyes, with an apathetic smile on their lips.

Some lean down toward me, whispering half-forgotten sweet nothings in my ear; others are lost in thought and don't notice me at all; still others laugh mockingly, and I feel as though at any moment they will hurl terrible insults in my face. But love, apathy, or mockery cannot touch me anymore.

I lie awake with open eyes during sleepless nights and look at them in cold surprise, and I seek to understand how these strange, distant people could have once been so close and dear to me. What magical thread bound me to them? And how had they severed that thread? And why was this all so alien and meaningless to me now?

They file past slowly and silently, and often I recognise my mother's footsteps among them.

She does not look gentle and unassuming as I remember her in my distant childhood, nor does she have her head held high as I knew her in her later years. She appears to me with that intimate, deeply tragic expression my memory has kept safe.

She looks at me and does not see me. Desperation—without solace, without hope—fills her wide, dark eyes, and a smile of infinite contempt burns over her pale lips, which seem ever on the point of opening, on the verge of releasing their terrible, momentous truth.

What was she trying to tell me?

Did she want to say that life was empty and grey, pitiless in its ordinariness? Like a wicked serpent life wraps its coils around your airy dreams and winged desires, smothering them with its venomous breath, killing them on the spot before they have a chance to bloom. Your struggles will be in vain, your attempts to free yourself from the ordinary, to rise above—life will ridicule and crush you without mercy.

Is that what she wanted to say?

Or did she want to say that love is small and ephemeral?—A pale spark against the dark backdrop of life; flashing but for a moment, only to vanish in the thick darkness? It cannot open up cloudless, starlit skies; cannot pour blue light over the cloudy paths of life. It is easily extinguished with only a little water; even its purist flame does not burn eternal.

Is that what she wanted to say?

Or perhaps she wanted to remind me that however beautiful and jubilant life can be, however brightly the sun of love can shimmer, embracing you with its gentle rays, there will always be, standing behind your shoulder, a merciless enemy as old as life itself—death. It stands behind you as you stretch out your hand toward the happiness calling out to you nearby; as you lie in the arms of your ardent beloved and dream of eternity; as you begin a great project and in passionate desires see it through to its end—it is always there behind you, with a cold smile on its bony face, ready to steal away your life, your love, your creative accomplishments—

What was she trying to tell me?

Signed: Khave Gross, 1909

At a Ball
אויף אַ באַאֶל

At a Ball

I SET OFF TO THE BALL in the best of moods. That day had been kind to me: it brought me a letter from a small woman with placid chestnut eyes. Before I began this year languishing in boredom in the provinces, I had bestowed upon her many merry little poems and sad glances. In return she had unexpectedly bid me a cold farewell and left for a distant city. Now she writes that everything—the farewell, the change of scenery—was all an attempt at forgetting me. A failed attempt. She can no longer bear to live without me. Her love is great and eternal.

Great and eternal, bah! That's taking things too far. Nevertheless, one may take pride in even such trifling victories as these. And so it was with a light heart that I set off for the ball.

I came late to the dances. In the provinces people dance with passion and heated fervour, but too earnestly, with too much intent, as though fulfilling a sad duty. And so I made my way to the side room where the youngsters engaged in a game of Flying Letters, that charming childlike pastime for adults of passing anonymous notes.

"Flying Letters," how fitting the name! Notes of blue, pink, and red take flight, often toward unfamiliar girls, whispering God knows what foolish nothings into their ears.

And the girls, stiff and taut—just try to say a word to them and they'll take your measure in a glance—those proud girls sink their hands into the pile of notes with greedy eyes, seeking, finding, and rejoicing. Like petals the mischievous confetti in their hair sparkles, and they laugh amid the merry embrace of serpentine ribbons.

I had only intended to be a spectator tonight. Though I have taken a vow to remain faithful to my future lover—a small woman with quiet eyes—I have nonetheless taken great pleasure in observing the young little ladies in bright soft rustling dresses. And if I am indeed to confess: I have kissed more than one of them in my thoughts. But only in my thoughts.

And at this point my gaze falls upon a girl.

She is young, but by no means beautiful. A large head perched atop a long neck, narrow, grey eyes. A freckled nose drooping gloomily down toward fleshy lips.

She is not beautiful, that girl.

She sits alone, up against the wall, and seems to be studying her opulent white fan of ostrich-feathers. Her face betrays a stubborn maliciousness, poorly hidden under the calm of good manners: the feigned apathy of one to whom life is apathetic. Who would not recognize her at once?

I turn away. Once again my fantasy embraces pretty girls, showering them in tender words with regal clemency until, unwillingly, my gaze is drawn back to that girl.

Her mask of cold propriety falls away bit by bit. The fan . . . *the devil take the blasted thing!* She hurls it onto a nearby chair. She is angry, she is enraged. It pains her—not a single note has landed in her lap. No one calls out her number. 78 is her number, I notice.

An idea flits through my mind.

I take a pencil and write:

"So long, so passionately, have I sought you. But now you will not escape so easily. My love will find you."

I seal the edges of the paper, write the number "78" on top and drop it into the box.

Fly, little note, fly.

A little later, the breathless young letter boy calls out: "Number 78!"

She lifts her head, appearing puzzled: Do they really mean her? Can it be true? Naturally her hands began to tremble as she takes the note.

She reads it slowly, perhaps for several whole minutes. Her eyebrows—her eyebrows are the only part of her that are indeed beautiful—pressed together. She shrugs, suspicion in her eyes. Ah, it seems this girl is no fool. She suspects some prankster is making fun of her, eh?

This irritates me, and so I write again:

"I am no stranger to you. You met me once by chance, and as chance would have it (or so I choose to believe) you did not notice me. And so I went quietly away, taking with me my dream of you.

You are kind. You will also allow me to say:

You who are so wonderful and proud, I love you."

She glances around, flustered. *Who is it?* her bewildered gaze asks. *The slim doctor in pince-nez? The young merchant with the golden chain over his waistcoat? Perhaps the brooding student with the long hair?*

But each is occupied with his lady. She begins to scan over the lonely faces of who can be found, one more or one less, at every soirée. I too fall under her watery gaze. In that moment I present a dull, apathetic expression. Her gaze glides on. When I sneak a glance at her my first impression: she has her doubts still, but she is starting to believe.

The more notes the letter boy brings her, the stronger her belief grows. The hostility frozen on her face begins to thaw, growing softer until it melts entirely, as though it were never there. She snatches my improvised love notes with enthisiasm, drinking them in, it seems, before even reading them. When she eventually opens them she reads slowly, hiding behind a seemingly negligent smile, with a dash of ridicule. She looks around the room, pleasantly fatigued, until, unable to contain herself, she takes the note out and reads it again carefully, earnestly, until the next one arrives.

She has given up looking for the sender of these tender, ardent words. In the end isn't it all the same? As long as the words keep coming.

And they keep coming.

I write on:

"I will not come to you during the commotion of

the ball. But later—and the day is close—I will come to you, and I will lay my love down before your feet. Do not reject it. Do not tread on any flower. My love is a flower."

I watch as the words exhilarate her. I rejoice alone in my corner. This must be how an artist feels when he conjures, at his whim, any melody he pleases out from inside one's soul.

Again, in a few minutes:

"You don't see me. What do I matter to you? But I am watching you from afar and kneel before your pride, before your lonely beauty..."

And the girl? She is intoxicated! She believes everything now. She even believes that she is beautiful. Her narrow eyes light up with happiness, with unnatural happiness. Her cheeks are flushed. Drops of sweat force their way out through her thick makeup. Even her melancholic nose seems to blush. She is now repulsively ugly.

And in that moment I write:

"You beauty, you enchantress..."

Signed: Khane Barit, 1914

Sources

"From a Diary": Khave Gross, *Di Tsukunft*, 1909.

"During Sleepless Nights": Khave Gross, *Fraye Arbeter Shtime*, 6 February 1909.

"In France": Khave Gross, *Fraye Arbeter Shtime*, 27 March 1909.

"At a Ball": Khane Barit, *Fraye Arbeter Shtime*, 11, July, 1914.

Acknowledgements

Special thanks to Beila Engelhardt Titelman, Mindl Cohen, Sonia Bloom, Nora Gold, and Jessica Sequeira

Anna Margolin

Anna Margolin (1887–1952) was the pen name of Roza Lebensboym. Born in Brisk (modern-day Belarus) in the Russian Empire, Margolin moved to New York in 1906, where she worked as an editor and journalist for various Yiddish-language newspapers. Despite only publishing one full-length collection during her lifetime (*Lider*, 1929), Anna Margolin remains one of the most enduringly acclaimed poets in the Yiddish language.

But she also published literary prose under the pseudonyms Khave Gross and Khane Barit including the four stories collected here for the first time.

Margolin in English Translation

Drunk from the Bitter Truth: the Poems of Anna Margolin, Trans. Shirley Kurmove, Suny Press, 2005.

Daniel Kennedy is a translator based in France. His translations include:

Hersh Dovid Nomberg

Warsaw Stories, White Goat Press, 2019.

A Cheerful Soul and Other Stories, Snuggly Books, 2021.

Happiness and Other Fictions, Snuggly Books, 2022.

Zalman Shneour

A Death: Notes of a Suicide, Wakefield Press, 2019.

Isaac Bashevis Singer

Shammai Weitz, Sublunary Editions, 2022.

Farlag Press is an independent publisher run by a collective of translators and literature-lovers. We prioritise translations from stateless and minority languages, as well as the writings of exiles, immigrants and other outsiders.

We are a strictly for-loss company, though we are registered as a non-profit association in France.

www.farlag.com

Also Available

1. Moyshe Nadir *Messiah in America (A Drama in Five Acts)*
Translated by Michael Shapiro
144pp ISBN: 9791096677047

2. Miriam Karpilove *Judith: A Tale of Love & Woe*
Translated by Jessica Kirzane
146pp ISBN: 9791096677108

3. Zusman Segalovitsh *Tsilke the Wild*
Translated by Daniel Kennedy
292pp ISBN: 9791096677115

Forthcoming titles:

Sam Liptzin *She Sold Her Husband and Other Satirical Sketches*
Translated by Zeke Levine

Farlag Bilingual Series:

1. Hersh Dovid Nomberg *À qui la faute ?* ווער איז שולדיק
(Édition bilingue: yiddish/français)
Traduit par Fleur Kuhn-Kennedy
66pp ISBN: 9791096677085

2. Hersh Dovid Nomberg *Between Parents* צווישן טאַטע-מאַמע
(Bilingual edition: Yiddish/English)
Translated by Ollie Elkus and Daniel Kennedy
74pp ISBN: 9791096677092

www.ingramcontent.com/pod-product-compliance
Lightning Source LLC
LaVergne TN
LVHW052048070526
838201LV00086B/5123